i

ONCE ... AND ... AGAIN

A STORY OF TIMELESS, EROTIC LOVE

ONCE ... AND ... AGAIN

A STORY OF TIMELESS, EROTIC LOVE

J. M. Manchester

COVER ILLUSTRATION BY
J.M.MANCHESTER

Clackmann Press

Seattle, WA

Printed in the United States of America

Dedication

To my darling, darling …

Live! Live the wonderful life that is in you! Let nothing be lost upon you. Be always searching for new sensations. Be afraid of nothing.

—Oscar Wilde

1

June, 2000. They turned into Holly Lane and Olivia knew right away what was going to happen. She became swollen with anticipation and she could feel her vulvae rising and spreading. Her warm juices were starting to flow. She reached her hand over the car's shift column and placed it firmly, but lovingly, against and around Flynn's ready penis that was making a huge bulge in his soft dress pants.

Holly Lane was a short, beautiful, pine-tree-lined street in the wealthy town of Harrington which bumped up against Quanessett Bay. Olivia and Flynn did not live in Harrington. Flynn's job was to inspect buildings built by his employer, *Castle Engineers Inc.* and, as she often did, Olivia had ridden along with Flynn on his day's assignment. It was a gloriously warm and sunny day in New England. Flynn completed his evaluation, and as they drove down the Norman-Rockwell main street in quaint Harrington, Holly Lane beckoned to them. It was as if there were a sign at the top end of the street that blinked, "Flynn and Olivia, enter here." And they did.

The homes were set way back off the road and were mostly blocked from view by the tall, abundant pine trees. Even with the limited sightings of pieces of the mansions, it was obvious that only the very rich lived on Holly Lane. There was a cul-de-sac at the end of the short street which stopped at the top of a cliff and looked down on the bay. Flynn pulled the car over to the left side of the cul-de-sac and parked up against the thickest clump of the trees. It was like being in a protected semi-circle of lush, green velvet. There was no one anywhere on the street or in front of, or beyond, the cul-de-sac trees. The sun was flitting through the branches of the trees and made it seem as if there were stars dancing everywhere in the middle of the day.

Flynn and Olivia sat in the quiet for a minute or two and then Flynn, still with his obvious arousal, swung open his door, got out, and walked slowly around the back end of his new, bright-red Jetta and then alongside to Olivia's door. Flynn and Olivia were both visibly shaking. This was risky. It was broad daylight and this was a public, though very quiet, street. But the danger made it all the more exciting—they seemed to thrive on precarious and exposed love-making. Olivia grabbed Flynn's helping hand and she let him pull her out of the car. With their sweaty hands held tightly together, they walked over to the very edge of the trees in front of the car. And there, up against the gigantic, vivid-green fence of pine trees, Flynn quickly unzipped his pants, exposing his impatient, provocative, throbbing miracle. He hurriedly lifted up Olivia's skirt which she had worn to allow for easy access; he urgently pulled down her lacy underwear as she balanced herself against his shoulder; he released her panties from one leg, gently wrapped that leg around his waist, and, with a groan of ecstasy, entered the heaven that was Olivia's welcoming and very wet vagina. Her full and flowing skirt fell down over her standing leg

2

and hid the phenomenally joyful undertaking beneath. Their arms were wrapped around each other and their lips were locked tightly.

They didn't care that at any time someone could drive down the road; they didn't care that someone in one of the secluded houses might take an afternoon walk; and they didn't care that it was school-bus time and that kids might hop off the bus and come running happily and innocently towards them. Flynn and Olivia were lost in each other and in their gyrating, spectacular, in-and-out salutations. Flynn came, and, in release and in euphoria, he yelled loudly. It didn't matter. No one was there; no one heard; no one saw.

The lovers felt weak and fully spent, deeply spent—their genitals still hitched together as if Olivia and Flynn were one being. Olivia's labia were spread wide open and were up against Flynn's groin while what was important was tucked safely inside Olivia's beguiling and welcoming home. After what seemed like being forever in some fairy-land, some celestial place, Olivia and Flynn reluctantly released each other; Olivia removed her leg from around Flynn's waist. His appendage slid out and dangled limply; it was still dripping. They fixed their somewhat wet clothes and hugged each other longingly in joyful silence. It felt to Olivia like her entire self was inside Flynn's soul.

For several minutes before getting back in the car, they watched the sunlight putting on its show. The sun's rays were still gleefully playing with the tree branches, darting in and out among them and whispering to them, "Catch me if you can." It seemed as if the rays were celebrating Flynn's and Olivia's passion.

Soon, the lovers got back in the car and drove slowly back to the entrance of Holly Lane. As they did with all their intimate places, they seared the memory of this beautiful, special street—

their street, Holly Lane—into their hearts. They didn't know if they would ever be back and wanted to remember it always. They turned left out of Holly Lane and headed back to the town of Mason River, fifty miles away, where Olivia had parked her car at the, by now, familiar Webster's Restaurant. Minutes into the ride, Olivia was holding onto Flynn's once-again magnificently erect manhood which had escaped through his pants' opening. She turned her legs towards Flynn, opened them, and grabbed Flynn's right hand. She helped Flynn's fingers find their way home, and his fingers lived there the whole way back to Mason River.

2

May, 1964. After five years of marriage, Olivia's divorce from Peter Jensen was final. Ever since she had left Arizona a year before, Olivia Adams suffered daily, hourly, every minute, every second from severe depression. Her mind would not shut off. Half of her questioned her role in the demise of the marriage; half of her tried to figure out Peter's behavior. What had she done wrong? What could she have done differently? Was it her fault that the marriage had ended? Why had Peter been so deceitful? Why had he been unfaithful? Why hadn't she been enough for him? What else had he done that she didn't even know about? Why did he gamble? Who gets locked in a library overnight? Lies and more lies.

Three years into the marriage, a move across the country to Arizona, where Peter would attend graduate school, hadn't changed anything except for the outside environment. The desert was shockingly different from New England. Cacti everywhere, rattlesnakes in the yard, roadrunner birds scurrying here and there, poisonous scorpions, lots of sun, no humidity, sheriffs' posses, a holster on every hip, a gun in every holster, levis, cowboy boots, tumbleweeds. It was the Wild West. Olivia loved it and took to it like a bee to honey. The young couple rented a small, reddish, stucco house and Olivia felt this warm adobe-like dwelling would emit heat and warmth into their troubled relationship. She loved the desert flowers, the extraordinary red/golden sunsets, and the huge expansive skies with stars so close it felt like you could reach up and touch them. This was the change the young union needed, Olivia thought. That was, until a couple of months later when Peter's same old pattern emerged in some kind of sick, triumphant, I'll-show-you, I'll-do-what-I-want, I'm-invincible, macho kind of way. Peter's graduate work at the university hadn't gotten in the way of his philandering—so many pretty co-eds, so little time. No wonder he always wanted Olivia to pick him up, at the end of the day, on a back street; that way none of his new lovelies would see him with Olivia. While Olivia supported them both by working at the obnoxious car dealership with the aggressive, hound-dog of a car salesman, Peter spent his time seducing women. How many? She never knew.

Before that year's end, Olivia had given up trying to make the marriage work. At age twenty-four, she returned to New England, found a teaching job at a local high school, and tried to re-invent herself and her life. But she considered herself a total failure. It was emotional torture. All those uncontrollable thoughts that circled and snarled at each other endlessly in her head. She couldn't shut them off, no matter how hard she tried, no matter what she did. Her friends tried to help her. They listened and advised, all to no avail. Olivia left work every day almost in a black, opaque blur as questions wrestled and swirled around in her brain.

Why go home? There was nothing there. Why do anything? Why go back to work the next day? The mischievous, intriguing, teenage students in her classes at least helped her to get through the day. It didn't matter. It wasn't enough. It wasn't a life. Why couldn't she stop thinking about Peter? Yes, he had behaved badly; but he was handsome and charming and funny and smart. She didn't want to stay with him unless he would change, which didn't seem likely; but also, she didn't want him to be with anyone else. Besides, probably everything was her fault anyway. Why else would he have acted the way he had? She couldn't shut her brain off and didn't know how to make sense of any of it. This was a thought quagmire and a full blown depression that was heading in a very bad direction.

Olivia had been back in Mason River for almost a year when, reluctantly, as a new divorcee, she agreed to go with her friend and colleague, Carla Paulson, to New York City for a weekend. Carla had met Joshua Rossi, a boisterous, horny, and flirty pharmaceutical salesperson, at a local night spot in Mason River, and he had invited her to meet him in Manhattan for a fun weekend. He would be there with a tag-along friend for Olivia. Olivia didn't really want to go. She didn't want to do anything. It didn't matter whom she would meet, he wouldn't measure up to her Peter, even with all his short comings. He wouldn't be as funny; he wouldn't be as handsome; he wouldn't be as smart. What good would it do to go to New York to meet someone else when her heart was ripped in shreds? When she just didn't care. When she didn't want to get out of bed. When she didn't even want to live.

It wasn't as if Peter Jensen didn't have demons that contributed to his unacceptable, notorious, and destructive behavior. Put in a boys' home on a farm at the age of nine, when his struggling, divorced mother could no longer care for him, he was sexually abused—over and over and over again by the farm's manager—for at least three years until he was moved to a different children's home. This time it was a home run by the Sisters of Mercy. And even there, the Mother Superior seemed to have more than Peter's interests at heart when she called him into her office on a regular basis. He never admitted the sexual assaults to Olivia until over thirty-five years later, at a reunion of sorts. She had known about the boys' homes and felt bad that Peter had had to spend his childhood there, but she knew nothing about the abuse. How could Olivia have known? How could she have guessed? She had never heard of anything like that. Much to her own detriment, Olivia was a colossal innocent—a young woman with innocent ideas, innocent beliefs, innocent expectations, and innocent dreams.

When she met Peter, Olivia thought he was a carefree, honest, sincere, intelligent, gloriously tall, handsome, funny and fun-loving young man who was going places. And it didn't hurt that he showed up in his summer-white Navy uniform. He was a sailor with beautiful blue eyes and an engaging smile and he made her laugh. Like other young women of her generation, Olivia had expected, sooner or later, to meet her knight in shining armor. And she did, at age sixteen—while on a double date with someone else—and it was Peter. Except he wasn't a knight and his armor had all kinds of chinks in it. Having sex (no less outside the church in the bushes) with the wedding singer on the rehearsal night before their—Peter's and Olivia's—wedding was apparently Peter's idea of a pre-nuptial celebration. This extraordinary betrayal cut to the core of Olivia's now very sickened being. She had discovered this monstrous duplicity two years into their marriage when she found an incriminating note from the wedding singer shoved under the door to their apartment. Olivia would never get over it.   Would she ever find her pre-marriage, bubbly, healthy self again?

3

May 22-24, 1964. The weekend would be a critical turning point in Olivia Adam's life. The World's Fair had blown into Flushing Meadows Park in the New York City borough of Queens a month earlier. Its twelve story, stainless-steel Unisphere, that depicted the earth, fit nicely with the Fair's theme of the ever-shrinking global inter-connectedness. Joshua Rossi and his friend, Carl Mancini, were looking for some inter-connectedness of their own, all right, with Carla and Olivia. And that was all they were looking for. They were married men in search of free sex.

Olivia may have been depressed and heartbroken and she may not have wanted to live, but she wasn't stupid. It took only minutes and a few questions to determine that she and Carla had to get the heck out of there. They scrambled out of the mid-town bar and headed to retrieve Carla's car from the near-by parking lot. As unpleasant and potentially dangerous as this meeting had been, Olivia had actually woken up somewhat. Whether it was these two married men who infuriated her and reminded her of Peter's infidelities and of her divorce, or whether it was the city itself—its screeching traffic; people rushing everywhere; the flashing lights and neon signs; the tall buildings; the colorful and somewhat sketchy sidewalk vendors. Whatever it was, Olivia was suddenly awake.

"Now what?" asked Olivia with annoyance, as they sat in the car in the parking lot. She was awake, but she was also aggravated with Carla for coercing her into this trip to New York City and even more annoyed that Carla hadn't seen right through Joshua in the first place when she met him at the night club in Mason River. Most of all she was mad at herself for going along with it all.

"Where do you want to go? What do you want to do?" responded Carla.

"We need to find a place to stay tonight; it's already dark and it's getting late," snapped Olivia in a tone that more than hinted at her displeasure. "I have a friend who lives in Queens. Why don't we head there, maybe he can help," she added with a mix of anger and resignation.

The two women hadn't made any arrangements for lodging. It would all work out, Carla had promised, and they could decide where to stay once they were in New York City. But, it hadn't turned out as either had thought it would. Now they were trying to escape to a safer place, a more hospitable place than the bar in mid-town Manhattan where they had met up with the two would-be adulterers.

Jack Sharon was a high school friend of Olivia's who had been living and working in New York City for three or four years. Olivia hadn't seen him since before her marriage, but she knew at least that he was a trustworthy person and she thought he could help them find a place or maybe even let them crash for a night at his place. No, they hadn't reserved any lodging, but Olivia had been smart enough to bring along Jack's address and phone number

11

just in case. He was the only person she knew who lived in New York City.

"Do you have a map in the car?" Olivia asked Carla with a still-cool-icy inflection in her voice.

"Look in the glove compartment; I think there is a map of the Northeast in there," Carla responded in her unflappably, always sweet, sing-songy voice, as if there were nothing amiss.

Olivia opened the compartment and pulled out several papers including the car's registration and three or four tattered maps. In the stack, as Carla had suggested, was a map of the Northeast with an inset of New York City. Olivia unfolded the map, located the inset, and then re-folded the map so that New York City was the prominent focus. She laid it on her lap.

"Okay, now I have to figure out where we are. Is there a flashlight in here?" she asked as she poked around in the glove compartment some more.

"Hang on, I think there is one in my door pocket," Carla replied. She fished around among the pocket debris—crumpled up tissues; old, dead pens; moldy cracker crumbs; and a safety whistle—and grabbed her tiny blue flashlight. "Let's see if the battery is still working," she said as she pointed the flashlight towards the map on Olivia's lap and pushed the lever up. It was a dim light, but at least it was a light.

"Move it a bit further over," directed Olivia. "Where are we? What street are we on? What is that building over there?"

"Slow down," said Carla. "First let's figure out the street. Wait while I walk up to the corner so I can read the signs. I'll be right back." And with that Carla hopped out of the car, jaunted out of the parking lot, and headed towards the closest intersection, in the dark. It was almost 9 p.m.

In two or three minutes, Carla returned with the information they needed. "We are on 47th street and the cross street is 7th Ave. Can you find that on the map?" she asked Olivia.

"Wait a minute, I am looking; I am trying to find it. Oh, okay, I have it. And I can see LaGuardia Airport and I know Jack lives somewhere near there. This doesn't look too complicated. But I will have to call him first before we head there to see if he is even home. There's a pay phone over there across the street near that theater. I'm going to run over there and call." And with that, Olivia dumped the map on the floor and this time, SHE jumped out. She darted across the busy street, leaping in front of cabs in a seemingly very careless way. But she made it across in one piece, slithered into the well-worn, defaced, dirty, smelly, and probably germ- and disease-ridden phone booth and made the call.

Ringggg, ringggg ringggg. Olivia started to worry that no one was there. There was so much city noise it was even difficult to hear the ringing. Then on the fourth ring, someone picked up the phone and, in a somewhat scratchy voice, said, "Hello?"

"Hello," responded Olivia. "Is this Jack?"

"No, this is Flynn. Jack isn't home. Can I help you?"

"Oh, … well … I don't know. I am Olivia, a friend of Jack's from Mason River, and I am here in Manhattan. My friend and I came for the weekend, but don't have any hotel reservations. We need to find a place to stay tonight and we don't want to stay here in the city. It's too expensive," replied Olivia. She wasn't about to tell this unknown person the whole story of what had really happened and why she and Carla didn't want to stay in Manhattan, although it was true that it was too expensive for them.

13

"We were wondering if Jack knew of a place near him where we could stay." Olivia guessed there wouldn't be a chance of free lodging at Jack's since he wasn't even there.

"I am sorry Jack isn't here, but The Traveler's Inn is right in our neighborhood and their rates are reasonable. Why don't you come to our apartment and I will direct you from here. Do you need help with directions to our place?"

"Oh, thank you so much," Olivia sighed with relief, "that sounds like a good idea. I have a map and I think I can see the right way to go. It doesn't seem too complicated. Do I have the right address—26-17 23rd Ave?"

"Yes, that is the right address. Your best bet is to go over the 59th Street Bridge ... wait, do you have a pen and paper?"

"I do, go ahead," she replied as she pulled a small pad and pen out of her pocket-book and wiggled carefully into a position where the street light was shining the brightest. She did her best to hold the phone, balance the pad while writing, and keep from bumping against anything in the filthy cubicle.

Flynn spieled off directions, hesitating between each part so that Olivia had time to write them down. "Take the 59th Street Bridge, ... then turn left on Northern Boulevard, ... turn left on 31st Street, ... turn right on Astoria Boulevard, ... go to Grand Central Parkway to 94th Street, ... turn right on 94th and left on 23rd Ave and we are on the left. Our apartment is on the first floor."

Olivia had managed to get it all; she thanked Flynn, hung up the phone, and dashed back across the street to the parking lot. "Okay, I have the directions and there is a hotel near Jack's apartment where we should be able to stay," she said bluntly to Carla. "Let's get going. I will direct you, just let me have the flashlight so I can see what I wrote."

An hour later, after getting off course a couple of times, they arrived. Twenty-third Ave was a street of two-story brick row houses, all connected, all looking the same, but each one different in some way from the next. Most had eight or nine steps that went up to a small landing with a railing; some had overhangs to keep out the sun and rain, some didn't; some had carports, others just driveways. Olivia and Carla found the number, parked the car in Flynn's driveway, got out, climbed up the steps to the porch, and rang the bell. Flynn opened the door and invited Olivia and Carla in.

Olivia noticed Flynn right away; that is, Olivia *noticed* Flynn right away; even in her depression and self-absorption, Olivia noticed Flynn. He had a welcoming smile, reddish hair—what there was of it—and he was wearing casual chinos, horn-rimmed glasses, a white, short-sleeve shirt and, most important, grey suede Hush-Puppies shoes. Anybody who wore Hush Puppies couldn't be all bad, Olivia was thinking. He looked to Olivia like a warm person. After introductions and a bit of chit-chat and after Olivia had offered a truncated explanation of the whole Manhattan fiasco, Flynn directed them to the Traveler's Inn around the corner.

And then he added thoughtfully, or perhaps brilliantly, "If you don't have plans for tomorrow, would you like a driving tour of New York City? It could help make up for what happened earlier tonight." Flynn figured that since their original plans had fallen through, they might like an alternative, safer adventure.

"Yes," Olivia threw out instantly, without even consulting Carla. Truthfully, Olivia had forgotten all about Carla. She felt like she was alone in the room with Flynn.

"Great. Will it be okay if I pick you up at 10:30 tomorrow morning?"

"That will work, thanks; right now, it's been a long day and we need to get to the hotel. So, we will see you tomorrow," Olivia declared as she sort of pushed Carla out the door.

4

The next morning. Olivia found herself worrying about how she looked. She couldn't remember the last time she had cared. She was getting excited about seeing Flynn again and she didn't even know him. She changed her clothes twice, looked disapprovingly each time in the mirror, and then frantically changed them again. She was fidgeting and fussing with everything when the desk clerk called to tell them they had a visitor waiting in the lobby. Whatever she had on, it had to do. There wasn't time for another change. Olivia and Carla grabbed their pocket-books and headed for the elevator. As Olivia came off the elevator, she smiled eagerly at Flynn and she was pretty sure he smiled back. It flustered her.

"Good morning," Flynn offered with a joyful grin.

"Good morning," the women responded in unison.

"Are you ready to see New York?" asked Flynn.

"We are, yes." Olivia answered.

"Yes," replied Carla.

"Great, then let's go see the city." And with that he led Olivia and Carla out to his white Plymouth Fury, a car that he loved, that he had parked in front of the hotel.

Between the two women, Carla was the pretty one. She had beautiful, long, Scandinavian-golden hair and sparkling, deep blue eyes. And that wasn't all. She had an exquisite smile and a voice that was always dripping-sweet. She could have stepped right out of Vogue. She was the former cheer leader, the beauty queen, the homecoming queen. Olivia didn't think of herself as very attractive, certainly not as attractive as Carla, although she knew she had a dynamite figure. Even so, she was quite shocked when she was the one who got to sit next to Flynn on the front bench seat. Carla sat next to the door. Olivia was not sure how or why that had happened, but she was glad it had.

As Olivia wiggled over to give Carla room, she bumped up against Flynn's leg and something very strange and unexpected happened. It felt like lightning had struck her leg and the voltage was traveling through her body. She jumped slightly. It was like a zing, an electric zap. That was the only way to describe it; it was a shocking zing-zap that shook her usually clear-headed and in-control demeanor. She started to shake a little and even felt a bit dizzy. "Get control," she commanded herself. "What is the matter with you? For crying out loud, get it together."

It was a very hot, humid day, hotter than usual for May. They had only driven a short distance when Flynn turned to Olivia and asked, "Is the air conditioning okay where you are sitting? Can you feel it?"

"It's great, thank you," answered Olivia. And it was at that very moment, that very second, that very nano-second that Olivia Adams fell in love with Flynn Spencer. It wasn't just the caring way he asked the question and it wasn't just that he cared enough and was aware enough to ask the question. Depression or not, the combination of Flynn's thoughtfulness, his warm demeanor, and his Hush Puppies—and of course, the leg-zing-zap-shock-thing—spoke to Olivia's heart. She didn't know why, didn't care why. She thought she was going to hyper-ventilate. Her breathing started to sound really funny to her and she hoped Flynn wouldn't notice. She didn't want to look foolish, but she thought she was turning red. She chided herself some more to very little avail. She was losing it. She was feeling something, for sure, but it wasn't the air conditioning—more like the heat of a furnace.

Probably oblivious to what was happening next to him, although maybe not, Flynn pushed forward with his tour. He drove them back over the 59th Street Bridge into Manhattan to Columbus Circle, then up Central Park West to 97th Street, giving them the verbal tour as they drove along. Flynn pointed out the Tavern on the Green—the famous restaurant in Central Park—and then the Museum of Natural History. At 97th Street, they crossed through Central Park and Flynn turned right onto 5th Ave. All the way down 5th Ave, there were plenty of things to look at—the Guggenheim, the Metropolitan Museum of Art, Tiffany & Company, Bonwit Teller, FAO Swartz, Saks Fifth Ave, then to Rockefeller Center and St. Patrick's Cathedral. They continued down 5th Ave past Lord and Taylor, past the Empire State Building, on to Washington Square Park and over to, and down, Broadway. Flynn was in no hurry. This was a slow, deliberate ride.

Olivia was pretending to listen to, and even to be fascinated by, what Flynn was saying. Really, though, she wasn't hearing a word he said. She continued to try to calm herself and to keep herself from fainting, which she was prone to do when she got excited. Her heart was pounding and pounding and she was sweating from every pore in her body in spite of the air conditioning.

If anyone had asked Olivia what she had seen on the tour to that point, she wouldn't have been able to respond because she had no idea where they had been; all she could think about was that her leg was touching Flynn's leg and that the pulsating shocks kept happening. Thinking about it took over her brain and caused it to cease functioning altogether.

Flynn continued the tour as he drove through Lower Manhattan and Greenwich Village down to Battery Park. He drove into the parking area, found a space, and turned off the engine.

"Let's get out and walk around. There's a great view of the Statue of Liberty and we can grab a quick lunch here."

As they walked around, Flynn asked, "How do you like it? Isn't she beautiful (as he pointed to the Statue)?"

"She is really beautiful," Carla agreed, "and so inspiring."

Olivia didn't speak. She thought her voice would crack. So instead, she smiled at whatever Flynn or Carla said and shook her head in agreement.

They stood for awhile looking out over the water of New York Bay and enjoying the breeze and the views. And then after a quick snack and a brief stroll around the park, they got back in the car and Flynn drove up the FDR Drive along the East River and crossed the bridge back to the hotel in Queens.

Flynn hoped out of the car and jaunted around the car to open the door for Olivia and Carla. They got out and all three stood somewhat awkwardly on the sidewalk.

"Thank you so much for the tour," Carla said to Flynn.

"Yes, thank you," Olivia chimed in, still in some kind of shock.

"You are very welcome," responded Flynn. "If you don't have plans for this afternoon and evening, I would be happy to show you around the World's Fair. It's right here in my back yard," Flynn said as he pointed in an easterly direction. "I have special access to the exhibits since it's part of my job to inspect them."

Olivia and Carla looked at each other for a minute, shook their heads in agreement and Olivia declared excitedly, "Yes, that would be great. Are you sure?"

"I'm sure, Flynn answered. "How about if I pick you up in an hour?"

"That would work," replied Olivia with her body starting to shake again.

"Okay," Flynn responded with a grin on his face, "bye for now. See you in an hour." With that he jumped back in his car and drove around the corner to his place.

After several lively and pleasant hours at the Fair with Flynn, after a quiet night at the hotel, and after a quick breakfast the next morning, Olivia and Carla said goodbye to New York City and headed back to Mason River. It had turned into a very, very unexpected, strangely happy, wildly fortuitous, and forward-looking weekend for Olivia.

5

June 26, 1964. It was a hot, steamy summer night in the Astoria section of Queens. Flushing Bay was on fire. The blue, green, red, and yellow lights from the World's Fair lit up the water to make it look like an inferno. The moon's rays joined in the fiery spectacle.

Flynn pulled into the small parking area that butted up against the water of the Bay. He quickly found a space and turned off the engine. There wasn't any privacy at Flynn's apartment with Jack there, so Flynn had driven Olivia to the Bay where they could watch the lights and talk.

Olivia was in New York for the weekend at Flynn's invitation. Their friendship had been blossoming since that infamous New York City trip. There had been birthday roses and a card for Olivia and there had been several phone calls from Flynn after that adventure. Olivia wasn't the only one who had felt something.

"This is magic," Olivia commented about the view. Flynn put his arm lovingly around Olivia and then moved his right hand up against the back of her neck, bent into her, and kissed her for what seemed like a very long time. This kiss had been waiting and wanting to happen since Olivia's leg first bumped up against Flynn's in his car a month before.

As their lips released, Olivia confessed, "Flynn, wait, I have to tell you something."

"Go ahead," he said. "I am listening."

Olivia took a deep breath and blurted out, "I am divorced, and I wanted you to know before we go any further." She didn't know what compelled her to do that, but she had said it and she instantly wanted to retract it. She had no idea what kind of reaction Flynn would have and was quite afraid it wouldn't be a good one. She was completely flustered. Had she ruined everything?

But Flynn didn't jump away; he didn't flinch. "Tell me what happened," he asked of Olivia. "Tell me whatever you are comfortable with."

"Okay," she replied. "I will try to explain it to you." And she began. "I met Peter when I was sixteen and he was nineteen and we dated for three years before we got married. I thought he was my Prince Charming, but it didn't quite turn out that way."

And so began a two hour, lopsided conversation—Olivia talked, Flynn listened—up against Flushing Bay in the Plymouth Fury. Flynn kept his arm around Olivia's shoulder and, if anything, he held her more securely as if to protect her from her own words, her own story.

When Flynn did speak, it was always a caring and encouraging comment. At one point, Olivia started to cry. Flynn reached across her and got some tissues out of the Kleenex box in the glove compartment. He wiped her warm tears gently and then kissed her again; it was a very tender, caring kiss as if to say, "Don't worry, I am not going to let anything happen to you."

But the more Olivia spoke, the more spent she became. "I think I need to stop for now," Olivia whimpered in a quivering, weak voice. "Can we talk more tomorrow night?"

"I'm here whenever you need to talk," Flynn responded with a genuine concern for her well-being.

They drove back to the apartment with Olivia resting her head on Flynn's shoulder. Once back, they snacked on a bit of cheese and crackers and then said goodnight with another sweet kiss. Flynn went to his bedroom which he shared with his roommate Jack, who was sound asleep, and Olivia slept on the living room couch. She was exhausted; reliving her marriage nightmare had drained her.

The next day was another full day at the World's Fair. And that night they returned once again to the parking area at Flushing Bay. The lights were just as sparkly, the moon's rays bounced around, and the night was steamy once again.

Olivia continued her story, her saga of what life with Peter had been like. Flynn did not disappoint. He didn't retreat no matter how deeply Olivia got into the betrayal, the hurt, her anguish. Flynn's calm and steady presence soothed Olivia and gave her the courage to continue with what she was saying, with what she had to divulge about the details of her painful experiences.

After another long, emotionally-charged session in the car up against the Bay, they talked about when they could see each other again. With the decision made, they returned to Flynn's apartment as they had the night before. With jumbled up thoughts of Peter and Flynn, Olivia drove back to Mason River the next day.

6

July, 1964. Barbra Streisand had opened in the new Broadway musical *Funny Girl* in March, and on July 25, during Olivia's next visit to New York, Flynn surprised her by taking her to see the show at the Winter Garden Theater. Once serving as a horse exchange, the building had decades before become a theater that was made to look inside like an English garden. Before the show even started, Olivia stood in awe looking in every direction, first in the lobby and then inside the venue itself. The colors and fabrics on the wall and ceilings were beautiful and cheerful and bright. Olivia's eyes wandered and gazed every which way. It drew her in.

This was Olivia's first Broadway show and she loved everything about it—the beautiful theater, the music, the talent, the costumes, the performance, watching the other theatergoers, and especially sitting next to Flynn and being part of this amazing event with him. She was in awe and so grateful to Flynn for getting the tickets. She didn't want the show to end.

The music, the lights, the whole experience would not leave Olivia's head and all together were much better company than the still-stagnant, controlling, detrimental thoughts of blame connected to the failed marriage to Peter. It was a welcome reprise from the almost constant brain barrage of negativity and guilt.

Flynn and Olivia drove back to Flynn's apartment in Queens. The thing that Olivia loved best about Flynn's car was that she could sit up close to Flynn on the bench seat and let her body touch his. She felt safe and secure whenever they were in his car. She put her hand on his leg and he covered her hand with his.

"I am glad you liked the show," Flynn said as he turned to Olivia with a big smile.

"I didn't just like the show, I *loved* the show," Olivia replied as she leaned into Flynn. "I can't get the songs out of my head. My favorite is *Don't Rain on My Parade.* I'm going to make that my new motto. I want my life to be as *juicy* as the song says and I want to be able to get rid of all the bad thoughts in my head so I can have that good life. I don't want anything, including an awful marriage, to rain on my parade."

"A juicy life would be good," said Flynn smiling. Little did he know that Olivia was already very juicy where it mattered.

She wanted to touch Flynn everywhere and couldn't wait to get back to his apartment. As they pulled into his driveway, her juice production quadrupled. Olivia was ready.

It was dark inside which meant Jake was not at home. That was a good thing. They barely got in the door when, in the dark, Flynn swung Olivia around to face him and kissed her. He started to undo the buttons on her blouse. She didn't stop him. He undid the top button and the next button, and when he had undone the third button, he reached his hand inside the blouse and inside her bra, cupped her breast in his hand, released it from its prison and started to stroke her nipple which responded by getting taller and harder.

"Ooooooooh," Olivia moaned in joy. *"Oooooooooooh,"* again she wailed. Flynn bent his head down and put his tongue on her nipple and ran it around and around. *"Oooooooooo, please keep doing that,"* pleaded Olivia as she tipped her head way back.

Flynn's tongue continued to swirl around her nipple and breast while his hands undid the rest of the blouse buttons. He put his mouth around the top part of her breast and began to suck lightly. At the same time, after he had pulled her blouse off, he unhooked her front-latched bra, slipped it off her shoulders, and let it fall to the floor. He then pulled her skirt and underwear down below her knees. It was amazing what Flynn could do with his mouth clinging to a breast. Olivia was groaning more and she thought she would die from the ecstasy.

Her vulvae started to swell more and bounce—back and forth, up and down, so swollen, so wet, they seemed to have a life of their own. This had never happened to her before. She was losing control and it felt good. She grabbed Flynn's hand and moved it down to where she needed it to be.

She stepped out of her skirt and underpants, now completely naked, and pulled Flynn over to the couch with his mouth still sucking at her breast. She sat down on the edge of the couch and at the same time, she pulled him down. He got on his knees next to the couch, slowly removed his mouth from Olivia's breast, raised his head up, and put his lips on hers ever so gently.

Suddenly, Olivia stiffened and cried, "Wait. What if Jack comes back home?"

Flynn had trouble even talking. His readiness was huge and poking and jumping towards Olivia. He managed to say in a shaky voice, "I doubt that he will. He is upstairs with Sherry and once he goes to her apartment, he usually stays for the night. But I will make sure he can't surprise us." Flynn reluctantly removed his hand from Olivia's home, got up off his knees slowly, and walked somewhat awkwardly over to the door, as if he had a basketball between his legs. He pushed the deadbolt over and, for good measure, hitched the security chain. A slim streak of light from the street came through the side of the front door window shade and lit Flynn's way back to Olivia. The apartment was still dark.

"Now nobody will interrupt us," Flynn said as he got back to Olivia, and once again he was on his knees up against the couch. He put his hand back where it had been and put his lips back on hers. Olivia felt safe now from any unexpected intrusion. She interrupted the kiss and peeled Flynn's shirt up over his head and started to kiss and suckle at his nipples. Her hands found Flynn's pants, moved up and over the lump gently, released the snap on his jeans, pulled the zipper down, and then grabbed the jeans and yanked them down to his knees. Out and up it popped. It was always ready. It was always hard. It was always moving. It was always searching. When it was around Olivia, anyway.

7

Peter Jensen. In the four years of marriage to Peter Jensen, nothing like this had happened to Olivia. And during their three-year courtship before getting married, Olivia had stayed innocent, very innocent. It didn't seem all that difficult to do. She didn't even let Peter touch her breasts, never mind anything else. Kissing and hugging were the limit.

As for Peter, there was one time at the end of a date with Olivia when he had had a problem. Peter and Olivia were sitting on the couch in the living room, after Olivia's parents had gone to bed, and were kissing and involved in light petting, which meant that Peter was rubbing her legs. Peter was wearing his Navy uniform (and there is nothing more pleasant to look at, thought Olivia, than a tall handsome man in a Navy uniform) because he had to return to the Navy base in Newport by 5 A.M. the next morning or be AWOL. In the middle of the kiss-fest, Peter suddenly came in his pants. That actually excited Olivia—Peter coming in his pants; the idea of having him come inside her didn't arouse her at all. Peter had to leave to be back to the Base on time, so with his pants filled with white goo, he said good-bye, got into his car, drove a little way down the street where there were plenty of trees, got out of the car, took off his pants and then his underwear, and threw the underwear into the bushes. He put his pants back on and drove off. They never spoke of it again.

Olivia's and Peter's wedding night was a harbinger of the train wreck of a marriage that was to follow. If Olivia were truthful with herself, she would confess she didn't even want to get married. By this time, she was in college, she had big career dreams, innocent career dreams. But towards the end of their three years of dating, Peter had started to put a lot pressure on Olivia. It wasn't overtly to have sex. It was to get married. Had Olivia been a little less naive, she would have known that the pressure to get married was really code for having sex. Peter wasn't going to get it short of that. In a final attempt to end the pressure, Olivia had said okay to getting married, and so they married two months later. She was nineteen; Peter was twenty-two.

Peter had gotten out of the Navy and both Peter and Olivia were now college students. They borrowed a car from a friend, these two kids, really, and drove to the Poconos Mountain resort area in Pennsylvania. In the room that first night, Olivia felt fright but not much else. As they stood in the middle of the room, Peter rather awkwardly removed her clothes, put them on the chair in the corner, looked for a long time at her body, fondled her breasts, and told her that her breasts were beautiful. He took off his own clothes, put them on top of Olivia's clothes on the chair; and he grabbed her hand and led her to the bed. They got on top of the bed clumsily. Peter had long legs that seemed to go on forever and always get in the way. He was over six feet tall. He climbed on top of her, tried to figure out where his legs should or could go, and then kissed her for a long time. He tried multiple times to penetrate Olivia and couldn't. Olivia started to sob because it was hurting. She found no pleasure at all in this and just wanted it to be over. Finally, Peter got in and a trickle of blood was released. He came quickly and Olivia just felt glad it was done; she didn't feel anything else. She turned over on her side quickly and pretended to fall asleep. She didn't want to go through that again.

For the rest of the marriage, the love-making, if you want to call it that, was lackluster, especially after Olivia learned about Peter's infidelities. In five years of marriage—well, four really because she had left after four—she never touched Peter's penis, never wanted to. She never even looked at it. However, she knew Peter's penis was long and skinny, even when erect. She knew this because, although she never looked at it, never wanted to look at it, it was too long for her vagina; part of it always remained outside. Inside her vagina, Peter's penis rattled around in a cavity it didn't fill. It felt like a rod in a bucket. It didn't fit. When sex happened, it was bare-bones and it brought Olivia no pleasure. In every way, this marriage was a disaster.

8

Back in Flynn's apartment. In stark contrast, here Olivia was five years after that dreadful wedding night, in Flynn's apartment, on his couch with her fingers roaming over his amazing shaft. At the same time his hand was massaging, searching around in, and loving Olivia's gateway. His lips locked tightly but tenderly again with hers. Her fingers were moving up and down his penis in the slowest possible way—over the ridges, over the swollen veins, up to the smooth mushroom top, to the slit on top where there were dewy pearls of moisture. She wanted to know every inch of Flynn's astonishing, beautiful being. Around the tip her fingers went—round and round—spreading the syrup around and then back down the sides. Meanwhile, Flynn's fingers found Olivia's wide open tunnel and went in. He moved his fingers in and out while her fingers moved up and down. In and out, up and down, in and out, up and down.

Their tongues touched and danced with each other. The tongues played together, felt every part of each other's mouths. The tongues were gentle, sensual, longing, desperate, wanting.

Altogether now, in some magical rhythm, it was Olivia's fingers going up and down on Flynn's love-maker, Flynn's fingers going in and out of Olivia's lush and overflowing vagina, and their tongues moving in and out and around each other's mouths. There was motion everywhere. Up and down, in and out, around and around. Then the slow and deliberate pace shifted. Everything was getting faster and faster, exponentially more needy, completely urgent, and humongously frenzied and ...

Olivia thought she would explode. She had never felt anything like this. She was lightly groaning—not in pain, but in pleasure, in desire, in love. Her pelvis was humping up and while it didn't seem possible, Flynn's penis was getting even thicker, more robust, wetter, and obviously happier. She tugged on Flynn's leg, signaling that he should get closer. Flynn stopped what he was doing long enough to get up from his knees, yank his jeans the rest of the way off, and then gently get on top of Olivia as she fell back on the couch. They couldn't wait any longer, and for the first time Flynn's bubbling, bursting, burning desire got inside Olivia's blazing asylum. His desire needed no help in locating its destination. Internal radar led Flynn's wet thickness right to the entrance of the flue. Olivia's vaginal magnet pulled him, sucked him, right in.

It was a perfect fit. There was no extra space in her vagina. Overwrought and over-ready, muscular and full, Flynn filled every crevice and his tip touched against the end wall. Olivia and Flynn moved in rhythm—up and down, up and down, faster and faster—for what seemed like forever. They were somewhere in an outer stratosphere. Their tongues mimicked the motions. There was liquid everywhere in every mouth. The fiery explosion was huge and glorious for both. It caused Flynn to see blue; Olivia was shaking everywhere. It was like the grand finale at the 4th of

July celebrations, except that instead of being in the sky, it was inside Olivia. It made Olivia think that maybe those 4th of July finales were just metaphors; children should not be allowed at those festivities, she thought with a hint of glee.

Flynn put his head down on Olivia's neck and Olivia held him closely. "I love you," Flynn blurted out.

"I love you too," responded Olivia almost in a whisper. And with that they fell asleep as they were and didn't wake up until three or four hours later. They didn't want to undo their bodies so they just mumbled sweet things to each other and stayed like that on the couch for the rest of the night. It was the first time Olivia had made love, that she had really made love. There was no going back.

WATCH FOR VOLUME II OF

ONCE ... AND ... AGAIN